Mother Sun

and her Planet Children

Dedicated to my grandchildren and all children who want to know about the sun, the moon and the stars.

Foreword

Our Universe is wonderful! Yet how difficult it can be to explain to children! This book is designed to simplify the task of explaining our solar system to young children. The facts contained in the book have been researched from the latest available information and are basically accurate. No attempt has been made to explain asteroids, comets, meteors, meteorites, or galaxies. Instead, the explanations have been confined to gravity, the planets, stars, solar system, and the universe. This book is meant first to be enjoyable to children and secondly to be informative about the universe.

Copyright © 1991 by Story House Corp.
All right reserved. Printed in the United States of America.
Published by Story House Corp., Charlotteville, NY 12036

Mother Sun
and her Planet Children

By Sigrid Rahmas
Author and Illustrator

Mother Sun is a big, big ball of fire in the sky. She lights and warms our Earth.

Our Earth is a ball, too. It is one of Mother Sun's smallest Planet Children.

The Earth is always spinning around, but we do not fly off.
We do not fly off because we are smaller and are held to the Earth by the pull of gravity.

On a clear night we can see the Moon because light from Mother Sun is shining on it.

When our side of the Earth is toward Mother Sun, it is daytime. When we are in the shadow, it is nighttime.

If the Earth did not spin, it would always be daytime on one side, and it would always be nighttime on the other side.

As our Earth spins, it also makes a big circle around Mother Sun; and our Moon circles our Earth.

Mother Sun also has gravity. The Sun's gravity pulls on the Earth. That is why the Earth keeps going around Mother Sun and does not fly off into space.

There are millions of suns in the sky, big and small. They are called stars. We see them only as little points of light because they are so far away. The suns are twinkling stars.

Stars that shine evenly are planets and moons. They shine because some sun is shining upon them.

Sometimes our Earth is between Mother Sun and the Moon so we only see part of the Moon.

On some nights, our Moon and the stars are bright in the sky. We see them best at night because Mother Sun's light outshines them on bright days.

Our Moon seems big, but it really is smaller than most of the stars. It looks big to us because it is close to Earth.

Our Mother Sun has nine planets circling her. Most of these planets have moons going around them. These planets, their moons, and Mother Sun are one big family in the sky. We call this family the SOLAR SYSTEM.

Planet Mercury is the closest to Mother Sun, the next planet is Venus. Then comes Earth. Mars, the red planet, is next; then Jupiter, the biggest. Next comes Saturn with pretty rings around it. Far out in space is Uranus, then Neptune. Way out in space is little Pluto.

Mother Sun smiles happily as her nine Planet Children circle around her at a great speed.

Jupiter is the largest of the planets.

Next in size
is Saturn.

Uranus is third in size.   Neptune is a little smaller.

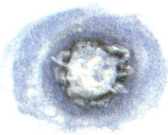 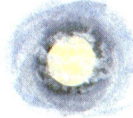

Earth and Venus are almost twins in size and are much smaller.

Mars is the third smallest.

 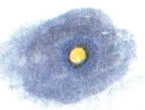

Mercury is next to the smallest.   Pluto is the smallest.

Mother Sun is much bigger than any of her Planet Children. She is the strongest. Mother Sun says to her Planet Children, "Gravity is a pulling force that we all have. We pull on things near us and we pull on each other. This pulling on each other keeps us circling, so that we never get lost or crash into each other."

Like our Earth, each planet has gravity. Jupiter says, "Mother Sun, you are very, very big; so you have more gravity than any of us. You pull more on us than we pull on you. That is why we circle around you."

Saturn says, "Our gravity makes us able to keep our moons circling around us. Some of us have many moons. Uranus has five big moons, and ten little dark moons that go around in an up and down direction instead of sideways."

Mercury says, "I am the warmest one of your children because I am closest to you. I go fast around you."

Venus says, "I have whirling air and thick clouds called atmosphere, just like Earth."

Earth says, "I get just the right amount of light and heat from you Mother Sun so that people can live on me. Animals, trees and flowers grow on me too."

Mars says, "I am the red planet. I am just a little farther away from you, Mother Sun, than Earth. I have two little moons and a pink sky."

"Next to you, Mother Sun," says Jupiter, "I am the biggest, so I have more force of gravity than any of your other children. Look! I have four big moons and twelve little moons going around me. I have small dark rocks whirling around me that look like rings."

Saturn says, "Even if I am only the second largest, I have a strong pulling force too. I am the prettiest of your children. My silvery rings are caused by millions of glittery icy rocks and dust whirling around me. I have twenty moons or more and every once in a while a new moon shows up among my rings."

Neptune says, "Mother Sun, Pluto, Uranus and I are very brave! We circle far away from you and you can hardly see us because of the mist around us. Pluto is so far away that he is almost invisible."

Uranus says, "Look at my fifteen-moons and eleven rings of rocks whirling around me."

Pluto says, "I have one moon and Neptune has two."

Mother Sun then tells her Planet Children, "You are all special to me, but there are many other suns and planet children in this big space called the Universe. The Universe has many Solar Families. We are just one of them. We are just a tiny part of the GREAT UNIVERSE."

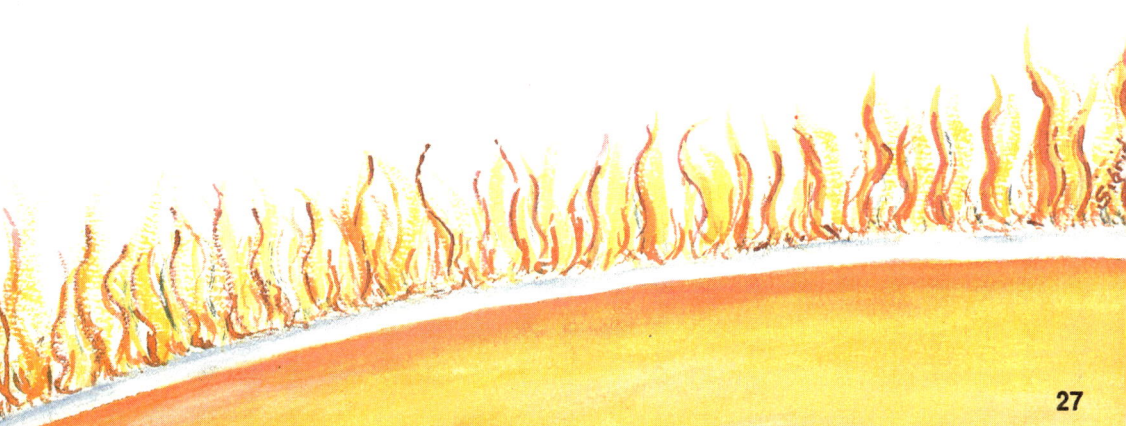

People on earth look at the sky through big magnifying glasses called telescopes which makes stars look bigger. The telescopes are in big buildings called Observatories.

Spaceships in the sky go by the planets and beam back pictures to T.V. screens in the Observatories.

Some people think there might be a tenth planet going around our Sun; but they are not really sure yet. Also, more moons are discovered around the planets from time to time.

Someday you might fly on a spaceship and discover planets and moons that are far away.

Planet Earth

Someday, if you do fly in a spaceship far into the sky, you will see that Planet Earth is a pretty ball with clouds going around it. Aren't you glad that you live on this one of Mother Sun's Planet Children!